Old King Cole

Old King Cole was a merry old soul,
And a merry old soul was he.
He called for his pipe
in the middle of the night
And he called for his fiddlers three.
Every fiddler had a fine fiddle,
And a very fine fiddle had he;
Tweedle dee, tweedle dee, went the fiddlers.
Oh there's none so rare as can compare
With King Cole and his fiddlers three.

adapted by Jeffrey B. Fuerst
illustrated by Nick Price

Old King Cole was a merry old soul.
He liked to laugh and play.
He liked to dance and sing, too.

One night, he went to bed.
But he was not very sleepy.

"What shall I do?"
Old King Cole asked.

Old King Cole called down the hall for his pipe. "Oh, Pipe! Get out of bed! Come here!"

His pipe got up and joined him.

Then Old King Cole called for his three fiddlers. They were playing cards.

"Oh, Fiddlers! Put down your cards!
Will you play a song for me?" he asked.

"Of course!" said the fiddlers.
"What would you like to hear?"

"I like the song that goes:
Tweedle dee,
Tweedle dee,"
said the king.

"We know that song!" said the fiddlers.

"Let's hit it!" said the pipe.

"Good song!" said the king.

So they danced and sang and laughed all night.